who's the
biggest?

This book will teach you how to describe size.
It's as simple as asking, 'Who's the biggest?'
Ask the same question on every page and see
what each pair has to say.

At the end, go back through the book.
Can you work out who's the smallest?

Have fun!

Delphine Chedru

who's the biggest?

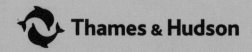
Thames & Hudson

"I am!"

trumpets the elephant to the butterfly

"I am!"

whispers the tree to the squirrel

"I am!"

grunts the bear to the honey pot

"I am!"

warns the hammer to the nail

"I am!"

murmurs the mountain to the bear

"I am!"

gurgles the fishbowl to my goldfish

"I am!"

hints the leaf to the ant

"I am!"

smiles the flower to the bee

"I am!"

booms the garden to the flower

"I am!"

giggles the cloud to the kite

"I am!"

hums the pan to the grain of rice

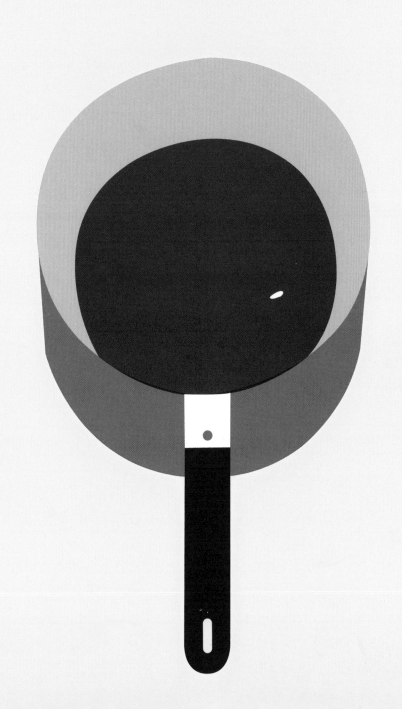

"I am!"

meows the kitten to my ball

"I am!"

sighs my umbrella to the raindrop

Who's the biggest?
Me or this book?

"I am!
I'm the biggest!"

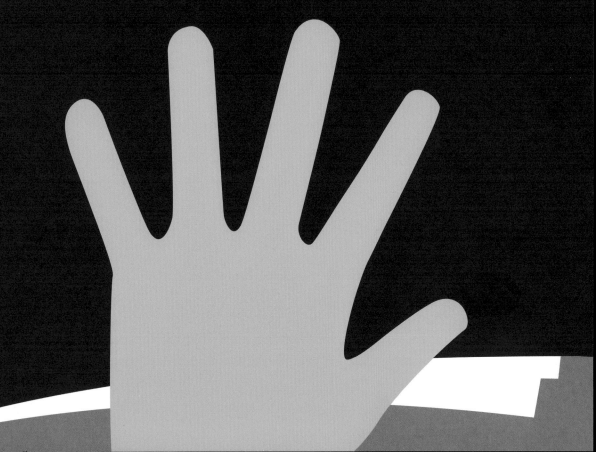

First published in 2018 in hardback in the United States of America by
Thames & Hudson Inc., 500 Fifth Avenue, New York, New York 10110

www.thamesandhudsonusa.com

Library of Congress Control Number 2017953044

ISBN 978-0-500-651490

Printed & bound in China by Lion Productions Ltd